# The Real
# Happily Ever After

# The Real Happily Ever After

*The Path to Her Destruction*

## Cherice King

Xulon Press

Xulon Press
2301 Lucien Way #415
Maitland, FL 32751
407.339.4217
www.xulonpress.com

© 2020 by Cherice King

All rights reserved solely by the author. The author guarantees all contents are original and do not infringe upon the legal rights of any other person or work. No part of this book may be reproduced in any form without the permission of the author. The views expressed in this book are not necessarily those of the publisher.

Printed in the United States of America.

ISBN-13: 978-1-6312-9082-4

# Dedication

To my beloved husband, Marques Dwayne Thomas. One day the Lord put it on my heart to write a book. When I would go visit Marques in the hospital, I would write, and I would ask his advice and get his input on things. He was always supportive of my book, my ideas, and my dreams. Also, he built up my confidence to accomplish my dreams. Moreover, he told me to go for it and that he was very proud of me. I love you always, Marques, and I will see you in eternity.

# Table of Contents

Dedication . . . . . . . . . . . . . . . . . . . . . . . . . . vii

Introduction . . . . . . . . . . . . . . . . . . . . . . . . . xi

1. Princess Erica's Moments of Tragedy . . . . . . . . .1

2. Troubled until Now . . . . . . . . . . . . . . . . . . . 13

3. The Punishment Your Sins Deserve . . . . . . . 22

4. Princess Met Satan Face to Face . . . . . . . . . 33

5. The Demons Were Abusing Princess Erica . . . 43

6. The Fall of Lucifer . . . . . . . . . . . . . . . . . . . 53

7. The Shame of the Queen's Daughter . . . . . . . .61

Author's Note . . . . . . . . . . . . . . . . . . . . . . . . 70

# Introduction

When you were a young girl or boy, did you believe in fairy tales? I know I did. I admired and looked up to Cinderella, Snow White, and Sleeping Beauty. They were awesome role models. They were every little girl's dream. Even my dream. These fairy-tale characters kept a positive attitude, loved unconditionally, and were very forgiving and humble. No matter how many times they were wronged by their enemies, they still had love and faith. Moreover, they had morals and values and didn't settle for less, but they kept one important thing out.... At the end of every story, the lady married Prince Charming, and they lived happily ever after. The End.

What amazes me about the fairy tales is that they always carried the nine fruits of the spirit but didn't represent the Spirit—Jesus. When I got older, Jesus revealed to me that these fairy tales show His nature through the characters, but they kept Him out of the picture while making sure to reveal the wickedness of demon creatures, witches, warlocks, fairies, etc. Instead of teaching girls and boys to put their faith in Jesus, these fairy tales teach them how to put their hope in fairies, witches, godmothers, and, mainly, themselves.

Moreover, I learned there is no "happily ever after" without Jesus Christ and the Father. The only way to live happily ever after is by accepting Jesus Christ as your Savior, and when you

*The Real Happily Ever After*

transition from this earth, your home is heaven for eternity. Now, that's the *real* happily ever after. This is a book everyone can relate to. If you've ever been through trials and tribulations, this book is definitely for you.

## Chapter One

# Princess Erica's Moments of Tragedy

During the midnight hour, Prince Charming's buddies were still having a pleasurable time with Princess Erica. They violated her in every imaginable way. They ripped her clothes off. They all raped Princess forcefully and beat her brutally. The boys spit at her, poured liquor on her, laughed at her, and called her every offensive name imaginable. Unfortunately, with the booze and different types of drugs in her system, Princess was completely out of it, and she had no idea what was going on.

**Princess's Experience of Death**

While these vile people were still violating her, she was snatched up in the spirit. In the instant of her death, her senses became heighten. All knowledge and understanding was quickly downloaded into her spirit. Princess now remembered what had led her to this point, and she knew what Prince Charming's plan had been all along and why he'd deceived her. She was looking down at her helpless body. She saw what those people were doing to her, and it sickened her. As she turned her head to the right, she saw Prince Charming sitting in an easy chair, enjoying the action.

## What Led Princess to Her Last Breath

Princess had been having a good time at Prince Charming's party, and now she was dead. Princess was partying with her friends and making out with her Prince Charming as well. Orgies and unnatural, detestable things were taking place at the party, and Princess was one of the contestants to attend. She was smoking a lot of weed and taking every kind of drug you can think of. As she was kissing all on the prince, he was secretly spiking her drinks to accomplish his plan. Disgustingly, under the direction of Prince Charming, she would make out with whomever he directed her to. The prince knew that the princess would refuse to do these awful things if she was in her right mind.

So the prince always had to made sure she was under demonic influences so she would obey his commands. Sadly, Princess Erica had no boundaries, and she lost complete control.

## Why Prince Charming Did It

Prince Charming directed this catastrophe for revenge. He was going to pay his enemy back at all costs. He had nothing personal against the princess, but she was the weakest link. He played with her emotions. Then he used her up like a piece of trash and threw her out to the wolves, as if he never knew her. The prince had to use someone dear to his enemy's heart so he could make sure they felt the same pain and hurt as he was feeling.

## Princess Was in Total Shock

Princess Erica, still looking down on the scene from above, rubbed her eyes and blinked, trying to convince herself that this wasn't really happening. She floated back down to her body, telling the people to get off of her and leave her alone. Nobody could hear her because she was now gone. What his friends were doing to the princess was unbearable for her to watch. She screamed at the prince, asking why he was doing this to her. Helpless and overwhelmed, she dropped to her knees and wept.

## Princess Erica Was on Her Way to Hell

While the disembodied princess was still on her knees, weeping, she noticed the atmosphere had changed. Fear enveloped her spirit. Darkness surrounded her, and she found herself in a long, eerie tunnel. Erica's heart began to beat rapidly. She noticed the presence of people in the creepy tunnel—people from all different nationalities and walks of life. Princess knew that at the end of that tunnel, there was something evil. So she got up and started to walk quickly in the opposite direction, but she noticed some type of force was blocking her. Princess fearfully turned around and started walking down the same path as the other people—toward the end of the tunnel.

She had no choice whatsoever. The closer she got, the darker it got. Swiftly she started to spiral down the end of the tunnel and fell flat on her face. Frozen with fear, the only thing Princess Erica could do was close her eyes. Princess Erica was now in hell.

## Everything Was Happening So Fast

Princess Erica heard the loud, terrifying screams of people being tortured. She was still petrified with fear, and all kinds of thoughts began to spiral through her head. Her life flashed before her eyes. She remembered all the times her parents had told her about the Lord, and she remembered that the

*The Real Happily Ever After*

queen had warned her not to leave the castle that night. She also remembered all the sins she'd committed against God without repentance.

Everything seemed to happen in the twinkling of an eye. She felt she wasn't ready to die and that this was not where she belonged. Princess didn't think her life would be cut short. She thought she had plenty of time. She was only seventeen years old.

## The Scenery and Horrid Smell in Hell

The sight of hell was horrifying, and the smell was undeniably gross. And the creatures that populated hell were worse than ugly. They were hideous! They were uglier than the ugliest animals on earth, and they smelled ten times worse than the smelliest.

And there were other smells there too. In addition to the nauseating smell of the animals, Princess was inhaling burnt sulfur, sewage water, and burnt flesh. She felt like she was suffocating because of the heat and the awful odors. There was no way to avoid the smell that filled her nostrils. She wanted to throw up, but all she could do was gag, because her stomach was empty. The horrendous sounds the princess heard in hell were very frightening. The agony and misery people were going through in hell was unbearable.

The princess felt severe pain as the heat burned her skin, and she wasn't even in the fire yet. There was no way to escape the nightmarish heat. There wasn't even any water for her to drink to quench her thirst. There were plenty of cages and lakes of fire everywhere.

The only light in the place was provided by the fire. Otherwise, she was in complete darkness. She couldn't imagine going through this forever.

## What Demons Used to Torture People in Hell

All of a sudden, two ten-foot-tall demons yanked Princess up and put her in chains. As the demons were dragging her along the ground, she saw what other demons were doing to the other people there. She saw people hanging on crosses, and the demons were burning them alive as they screamed in agony. There were bodies parts hanging everywhere. Furthermore, there was a place called the tool room. Demons were joyfully waiting in line to get those tools to torture and hurt their assigned prisoners. Princess saw all different types of tools to torture humans—chainsaws, drills, hammers, and screw drivers. There were plenty more wicked tools in that place, but Princess was allowed to see only those tools. Also, there was a sharpening stone where demons were taking turns sharpening their knifes so they could more effectively inflict pain on their victims. She overheard them laugh and gossiping about some of the people they had already tormented or were about to torment.

Dreadfully, she saw people in their cages being torture in all different kinds of ways she could never have imagined. The wicked things evil people did on this earth were nothing compared to what those demons were doing in hell itself. While they were grabbing her, Princess was constantly calling on Jesus, but the two demons just laughed.

They told her Jesus couldn't save her because He wasn't in that place. Furthermore, they violently push her down to the ground and told her that was her home now. It terrified her to know this could be her home forevermore.

## Princess Erica's Evil Ways

Princess Erica was very beautiful in her form but very ugly in her spirit for those who really discovered her true nature. Princess's physical nature was flawless. She had no outstanding

*The Real Happily Ever After*

facial features, but she was very beautiful. She had medium-length, soft brown hair and smooth, caramel skin, and her body shape was to die for. On the other hand, Princess's spiritual nature was evil. After Prince Charming popped her cherry, her demeanor changed drastically toward a lot of people, especially her parents. Eventually, Princess Erica began living a fraudulent lifestyle and moving quickly toward the point of no return. She started doing all different kinds of drugs, drinking a lot of alcohol, and robbing and scamming people, all because of a penis. She made a final decision that she was going to live her life her way. The princess had no idea she was playing with fire.

She took her life for granted, and she definitely didn't know she was going to hell very soon. The princess was well aware that if she didn't serve Jesus wholeheartedly, she would suffer the consequences. But she really didn't care at the time, because her body had been awakened by the seductive touch of the prince.

## Erica Tried to Hide Her Sins

In public, nobody knew she had walked away from the Lord, because Princess knew how to charm people with her glamorous smiles and gorgeous eyes to hide her sinful nature. On the other hand, the queen knew exactly what was going on, and she tried to hide the embarrassing behavior of their daughter from the king. She was horribly disappointed and wanted to know who took her daughter's innocence away. The queen hadn't revealed these things to the king, because she knew this would break his heart.

The princess was Daddy's little girl, and he could see her do no wrong—until something momentous happened.

## Princess Erica's Sneaky Ways

Right before dawn, the princess and her friends would go out, and they'd sneak into the woods when it got completely dark. The king knew nothing about it. He had issued a stern warning to the twins that, although they were allowed to go almost anywhere in the kingdom, they could never go into those woods. He had said plenty of times that it was dangerous, and someone could easily get hurt or killed.

According to him, the only way the princess and her friends could survive the woods was if Prince Charming or his mother was presence. There were always dark stories about the woods, about how people went missing there, about how some became slaves in that kingdom.

On the other hand, the wise queen knew Princess Erica and her friends were going into those woods, because the Most High had blessed her with the gift of discernment; she was a prophetess. The queen knew that evil spirits had taken over her daughter completely. The queen would constantly pray and decree over her daughter's life, no matter what she had seen. She had faith and she believed that the Lord would save her daughter one day.

## The Queen's Secret Was Making Her Sick

The queen had to revealed to her beloved husband what had happened to their precious daughter, Erica. She felt a push in her spirit to tell her husband, but she held back because of fear. She couldn't keep it to herself much longer, and it was tearing her apart. The queen had been sick for days, wondering how she was going to tell her husband this tragic news. She felt lost, angry, scared, and hurt at the same time. Honestly, it was difficult for her to pray. All she could do was say, "Help me Jesus," over and over as she wept. Her heart was broken. The queen was numb and weak. After a short

*The Real Happily Ever After*

meltdown, she decided to pull herself together and trust Jesus with all her heart. Hearing tragic news about their child is a lot on anybody. It doesn't matter how saved you are. So the queen made a request to visit the king in his chambers, and he agreed. As she was going to see the king, her heart was racing rapidly. Everything was going around slow motion but fast. She was getting very hot and dizzy. She felt like she was going to pass out. But she reassured herself that she had this.

## The Queen Had to Reveal the Bad News

What bothered the queen was that she'd never kept a secret from the king, especially not one about their children. Just the thought of holding this secret too long bothered the queen to the core of her being. As she got closer to the king's chambers, she felt butterflies in her stomach. She finally entered the room and respectfully bowed before the lovely king. He noticed that his wife was troubled. He grabbed her by the hand and lifted her gently to her feet, pulling her toward him and hugging her passionately.

She let all her emotions go and wept in his arms. He reassured her that she could tell him whatever was going on. Then he lovingly kissed the queen on her cheek. She revealed everything that had happened to their daughter. She said Erica had been sneaking into the woods and could possibly be in serious danger. The queen even told him about the dreams the Lord has been sending her to warn her about their daughter. The king was very hurt, and his heart was broken. But he held his feelings in to comfort and console his precious queen.

## The Noble King

Justice was a great king who loved the Lord with all his strength and with all his might. He was loving and very fair in judgment. King Justice was also very handsome and had gorgeous facial features. He had compassionate eyes and was very tall. His best characteristics were his humility and his gracious spirit. Even though the king carried a lot of grace and mercy, he definitely didn't let anybody run over him either. Without hesitation, he would rebuke anyone when it was necessary, but it all came from pure love.

The king was very wise in his choices because he put all his hope in someone that had greater wisdom than he, and that was Jesus Christ. King Justice had immaculate wisdom, and that was what made him great in his kingdom. Whenever he had to make difficult decisions, he consulted the Lord first for advice. The king knew he was nothing without Jesus and that all the glory belonged to Him.

## The King Had the People's Heart

Because the king put all his trust in the Lord, he became the most righteous and just king in all the kingdoms. That's what drew plenty of people to him. People were very comfortable in his presence. It didn't matter what you looked like, and it didn't matter if you were rich or poor. The only thing that mattered to him was the condition of a person's heart. He really cared about the people in his kingdom more than he cared about himself. He was also affectionate and a good listener. People felt they could tell him their darkest secrets and be themselves. This remarkable king always made time for people, no matter how busy he was. He joyfully served the people, and most importantly he was equally joyful in serving King Jesus Himself. Even though King Justice ruled, he never thought himself to be above anybody. He knew all things came from God, and he was thankful that Jesus even trusted him with this kind of position. King Justice loved Jesus and honored him deeply.

## The Beautiful Kingdom

This particular kingdom was beautiful, and, as an island, it was separated from all the other lands, and it was very pleasing to the eye. The kingdom was surrounded by crystal-clear, light blue waters. The sun glistened over the kingdom, making the waters shine like diamonds. The houses were big and elegant, and there was not a small house present. If the people of the kingdom found someone unfortunate, they invited them into their homes. Joyfully, the birds hummed pure, soft music, and the flowers and grass swayed back and forth to the music. Everyone and everything in that kingdom had joy and peace in their lives, despite what life may have brought their way.

## The Blessed Kingdom

Above all else, what the residents had was a peculiar kind of joy and peace like in no other kingdom. Nobody could remain sad or angry for too long, because the presence of the Lord was heavy in the air. They obeyed and loved the Lord with all their hearts.

Amazingly, there were rarely any worries, sicknesses, or tragedies in that land. The most pleasant thing about this kingdom was that everybody was welcome, and almost everybody that visited the kingdom left as a new person. Their spirits were stirred by fresh revelations that they'd never heard of before. People visited the kingdom from everywhere and wanted to witness to everyone what they'd seen and heard. Ultimately, these blessings were happening in that land because this kingdom was blessed beyond what the human mind could understand. It was the most prosperous and wealthiest kingdom in the land. The wonderful reputation of this kingdom spread like wildfire to all nations.

## Honoring the Most High

One amazing thing about King Justice was that he loved to give and to help others. He also taught his kingdom to not only give to others but to pay their tithes and offerings before the Almighty King. He believed that giving to God was the highest act of love, honor, and worship, and the Lord loved him for that. Last, but not least, he taught them that everything on this earth belonged to the King of Kings and that it's always important to give to the Most High God and to each other.

## Celebration Before the Lord

Every Sunday at noon, the people of the kingdom joined together in the town square and gave thanks and praise to the Most High King. The community was filled with the presence of the Lord and with much laughter. Even angels would come to give thanks and to praise Jesus. The air was filled with beautiful music and the scent of food. People brought dishes from their homes that fed the entire kingdom. Nobody struggled or lacked anything, because everyone was there for one another, and the protection and blessings of the Lord were upon them. Moreover, the sons and daughters happily sang and danced before the Most High, and He was well pleased. This kingdom partied before the Lord, and it brought joy to His heart. The Lord of Lords inhaled and soaked up every statement of praise, and He was comforted.

## Angels' Records of the Residents

There were all different types of angels present at the party and enjoying themselves. Angels loved to be in the presence of God, where there is praise and worship. They were happy because they had good news to report to the Lord. They had fun, but they also had their jobs to do. In this pleasant place,

*The Real Happily Ever After*

some of the angels were assigned to write down everything an individual was doing. They would report how much an individual gave in tithes and offerings out of their abundance or lack, how much food and materialistic things they had given to help others, what their attitude was when they gave to one another, what their true intentions were when they helped one another, and the praise they gave to the Lord. These things were always recorded.

*Chapter Two*

# Troubled until Now

On all the prior occasions when her daughter had gone out, the queen hadn't been too troubled. Now she was. For three nights, Queen Dawn's dreams had been awful. They seemed to be telling her that her daughter was going to be in serious danger on the coming weekend. Queen Dawn knew these warnings came from the Lord. As she was getting ready for bed, she kept seeing gruesome things for her daughter. In the spirit, she kept seeing people doing witchcraft and all other types of creepy things. Moreover, the queen was seeing creatures all over her daughter while she was screaming for help. They were growling at her, biting her, and digging their claws deep into her skin. The queen immediately woke up out of her sleep, and she knew her daughter was in danger. The Lord was giving her pieces of the puzzle to warn her what was ahead, but He didn't give her more than she could handle spiritually. The queen quickly got out of the bed to go talk to her daughter. Furthermore, she knew words were powerful, and the queen was wise enough to keep it to herself. After crying all night long, she pulled herself together and stayed focused on the Lord.

## The Queen and Princess Have a Disagreement

The queen thought it was time to warn her daughter not to leave that night. As the princess was getting dressed to go with her friends, the queen asked if she could come into the dressing room to talk with the princess. She sat down across from her daughter and looked at her. She marveled at how beautiful her daughter had become, and tears filled her eyes. She started to reminisce about when Erica was just her precious little girl.

Now she was all grown up and ready for womanhood. The princess had a rude look on her face, as if she knew what her mother wanted to talk about. The queen quickly wiped her eyes without the princess ever noticing. The princess urged her mother to make it quick, because she had to hurry up and go. The queen straight out asked her if she was having sex. Princess Erica was very surprised, and she became defensive. She reassured her mother that she wasn't having sex and that she was just having fun with friends. The queen asked what was going on with this smart mouth of hers and all this sassiness, for the queen knew that a man had been with her. She grabbed her daughter by the chin to let her know who was boss. The princess quickly got herself together.

## The Last Warning for Princess Erica

The queen reminded her daughter of all the consequences of having sex before marriage, and the princess looked at her as if it was gross to talk about such things. The queen just laughed at her because the princess was trying to insult her intelligence, not thinking that she was once a teenager too.

"If a guy doesn't respect you enough to wait, then he doesn't love you at all," said Queen Dawn. "Furthermore, if a guy is trying to get into your pants before marriage, he's definitely not from the Lord." She looked her daughter straight in her eye to let her know she was no fool. She was amazed that her daughter thought that the Lord wouldn't reveal things to her.

With an attitude, the princess told her mother it was none of her and God's business what she did.

The queen reached out and smacked her daughter right in the face. "The Lord is trying to save you from something. Now, you're not to go in those woods, or you might not come back."

"Whatever," said the princess. She grabbed her things and walked out.

## The Virtuous Queen

Queen Dawn was one of the prettiest women in the kingdom. There were definitely a lot of beautiful women there, but the queen had something special. What made her stand out before King Justice was her submissiveness, respect, and love for Jesus Christ. She also served her husband perfectly in every way. Queen Dawn was flawless, wise, and witty. And she was very successful and used her gifts and talents to bring glory to the Most High God. She had a gentleness and a sweetness to her, but she was a powerhouse in the spirit at the same time. She was a boss. Her inner beauty was more outstanding than her physical appearance, and she carried all the fruits of the spirit. Therefore, she was a virtuous woman and was loved and respected throughout the entire kingdom. All the little girls and young women looked up to the precious queen.

The princess, on the other hand, was no longer a virtuous woman at all, and the queen's heart was saddened by this.

## How to Be a Virtuous Woman Before the Lord

The queen had taught all the young women throughout the land how to become a virtuous woman before their husbands and the King of Kings. The wise queen taught them that being honest, humble, righteous, and respectful was far more beautiful than anybody's outside appearance. She taught them how to love the Lord with all their heart, mind, and strength. She also taught them how to love themselves and not devalue themselves, because they were worth more than they realized. Moreover, the queen taught the young women to love and be respectful of others in their daily lives. She taught them not to be desperate or anxious for things, especially for men, but to always be eager for the Lord. She taught them to always give thanks and praise to the Lord as well.

Last but not least, she told them that the King of Kings would eventually bring them the husband of their dreams and to stay focused on Him always. Therefore, the King of Kings loved them and made the queen prosperous in every way. The queen became well known for her reputation throughout the land.

## Princess Erica's Assigned Angel

Kayton's assignment to Princess Erica was to minister to her, lead her down the path of righteousness, and warn her when trouble was coming her way. Kayton's duties with the princess had faded away because she didn't listen to the Holy Spirit anymore.

Kayton would warn Princess from time to time, but she wouldn't listen. After losing her virginity, she spent less and less time with Jesus, and finally she completely stopped. Kayton was really sad that he'd lost Princess Erica spiritually.

Kayton was a beautiful angel to the eyes. He had big wings with soft feathers that had multiple colors blending together. They were the prettiest colors the human eye had ever seen. Kayton was ten feet tall, with long, curly dark blonde hair and beautiful green eyes. He had flawless skin, the color of bronze, covered with extravagant shiny green jewels.

*Troubled until Now*

## The Angel Reported to Jesus

Princess Erica's assigned angel went to heaven to report to the Lord about Princess Erica's loose lifestyle. He respectfully bowed before Jesus with reverence and fear. He reported that Princess Erica had closed her ears to the warnings he'd been giving her lately. He told Jesus the last warning had come through Erica's mother, and the princess was disrespectful to the queen.

Jesus was sorrowful in his heart because he saw something terrifying ahead that he definitely didn't want the princess to go through. Jesus told the angel that whatever happened to Erica had to happen this way, but He would not give up on her. Jesus gave people free will to make choices, and she'd made hers, despite all the warnings she'd received. Demons had been assigned to Erica as well. Satan had sent them to her at the moment of conception, and they'd taken over Princess completely. They got her where they wanted her. But Jesus remembered her mother's prayers and her father's loyal dedication to Him, and it touched his heart. She would have to endure whatever plans Satan had for her, but Jesus would have the last word.

## Princess Erica's Wrong Judgement

Prince Charming was waiting for Princess Erica and friends to joined them for this special event they had every other weekend. Once they met, they were ready to go through the woods. In reality, the prince cared nothing about the princess at all. He had his own wicked agenda in mind. To him, she was just another silly girl who was gullible and naïve. What turned the princess on about Prince Charming was his sweetness and kindness toward her, until she opened her legs for him. Unfortunately, she never really discerned the evil side of him because she was too busy lusting after his dazzling looks

17

and scrumptious flesh. She wanted to be in a relationship so desperately that she didn't want to wait on God to bring her the man who would be her better half. She was too deep into the prince, and there was no turning back.

## How the Princess Became Hooked

The prince made her feel wonderful sexually and emotionally—beyond anything anybody else had ever made her feel. The way he touched her, kissed her, and caressed her, and the sweet things he whispers in her ears, made her obsessed with him.

Eventually, she became his sex slave. He was her god, and she did whatever he wanted her to do. She knew it wasn't right, but she didn't care. Now the prince had her where he wanted her. She fell into his trap. She let herself go. Her self-respect and morals had gone down the drain because of lust, which she foolishly thought was love. Sadly, she had no idea that this wasn't going to last. She was hypnotized by this man's touch. The only thing she cared about was the moment—the right here and right now. She wasn't thinking of the consequences. This moment felt too good. She was in too deep, and she couldn't turn back.

## Erica Allowed Sin to Overtake Her

Whatever Prince Charming wanted her to do, she allowed, as if she were his slave dog, even though she knew it was wrong. Princess knew the ways of the Lord, but instead of following them, she allowed the desires of her flesh to envelop her soul completely.

What women failed to realize was that when they were practicing any kind of sexual sin, they were behaving outside of the will of God, and they became easy targets of the devil's tricks and schemes. Also, they lacked wisdom and discernment and became fresh meat. Princess Erica was operating under witchcraft because she opened the door to sin. She was in for a real surprise.

## Princess Erica's Vulnerability

Prince Charming knew the princess had never known a man before. When she first met Prince Charming, she was quite reserved and very shy. In the beginning, when he kissed her softly on her cheeks, she would giggle. If he caressed her thighs, she would have a silly look on her face. Prince Charming wanted to loosen her up a bit. So he took his time with her and played the perfect man he wanted her to be. Princess Erica knew she was immature at first, but now she was ready for Prince Charming to have his way.

Every time he would put his hands on her, her whole body would tingle. She'd never felt that way before.

The princess knew the consequences of committing fornication, but she let her body respond by instinct. She was debating with the Holy Spirit that she wanted to try it only one time, and then she would be a good girl again.

## Prince Charming Put It on Her

Prince Charming gently came behind her with his warm, muscular body. He seductively kissed her on the back of her neck. She felt every inch of his manhood thrusting on her gluteus maximus. Immediately, her honey pot got hot, dripping with honey. As he fondled her breasts, she moaned continuously. Then he slowly drew his fingers from her breasts down to her rose bed, and his fingers were smothered with the princess's vaginal juices. The touch of the princess's vagina had Charming's anaconda covered with cream. As this was going on, the Holy Spirit was warning the princess not to go through with it, telling her that it wasn't too late.

*The Real Happily Ever After*

Princess was far along in the game, and she didn't want to stop. She couldn't stop. She wouldn't stop. Now she was ready to open up her legs to satisfy his desires. He gently laid her down on the bed. He was rubbing his body against hers as he was passionately sucking and kissing her breasts. He whispered in her ear and asked if she was ready. She responded yes, with a sexy moan. She didn't know that she was about to become one, spiritually, with the prince. Whatever demons he was possessed with would become a part of her now. The prince gently pulled off her panties. He started to passionately kiss her from her abdomen straight down to her melting pot. The way he used his long tongue inside of her made her explode. As she was thrusting the prince's head, his tongue went deeper inside of her. At this point, Princess didn't give a damn about what her mother or the Holy Spirit said. She wanted him now. Princess started to feel vibrations, and then she let herself go.

## What Prince Charming Was Passing Along to Princess

The prince slowly slid his manhood inside of her, and she felt a bit of pain. He told her to relax and that he was going to take it slow. As she was enjoying the moment, his demons, the spirits he had sex with, and his sexually transmitted diseases were transferring to her. Princess was changing mentally, physically, sexually, emotionally, and spiritually. The prince was loving how his penis was enwrapped by her tight warm vagina. Now it was getting intense. He was going deeper and stronger. The prince's moans were getting louder. He whispered in her ear and told her how good it felt. At once, he ejaculated inside her soft cushion. Then he gently kissed her on her forehead.

Princess had now made a covenant with the prince.

*Troubled until Now*

## Prince Charming

The prince was more evil than both his parents combined. He was definitely conceded and had no respect for women because a lot of the women in the kingdom had no respect for themselves. Plenty of them threw themselves at him promiscuously, and he treated them like trash after he got what he wanted. Prince Charming lived a devilish and reckless lifestyle. He had beaten and murder people secretly, especially the Christians that lived in the poorest parts of the land. If anyone said a word to his parents, they were gone. Prince Charming was so treacherous and coldblooded that he got what he wanted, whether they assisted or resisted. He operated under witchcraft, just like his mother, but he went to higher levels than his mother ever did. He had no limits, and he hated his entire family, especially his mother, because her secrets had been revealed. Now Prince Charming wanted revenge.

*Chapter Three*

# The Punishment Your Sins Deserve

As the two demons were taking the princess to her cage, she noticed the tunnels she'd taken went to different levels and sections of hell. Whatever level of sins you were practicing on earth before death, that was the level you resided in forever. Princess Erica was on the level where people committed all types of sexual sins only.

There were sections for those who committed fornication, adultery, homosexuality, orgies, pornography, masturbation, lusting, and sodomy. There was a different punishment for each sin. The more sexual sins you committed, the more affliction was added to you. Princess saw demons raping the prisoners brutally in their cages, while other demons watched and took turns. In other cages, there were demons cutting off people's sexual organs and shoving them in their mouths while they choked and gagged on them. Furthermore, there were demons forcing sharp objects constantly into their sexual body parts. As they were brutally abusing them, the demons would cheer each other on and give each other high fives, enjoying the action. The people felt excruciating pain and

*The Punishment Your Sins Deserve*

bleed to death, only to come back once again. Erica could see the pain and agony on their faces, as if they wanted to die, but death refused to take them. After they were tortured, their body parts would heal so that they could go through the same affliction again for *eternity*. She cried silently as she watched these horrid things happening right before her eyes. The demons threw her violently into the cage. Then the demons told princess that she was very stupid, and they described how they'd tricked her to coming to hell. They told her Prince Charming worked for them, and they got her good. They laughed at the princess and told her she'd fallen into their trap. Her tears quickly dried up because it was extremely hot in hell.

## King Justice Walked with the King of Kings

King Justice was walking on the beach conversing with the Lord, which he enjoyed doing on a daily basis. Walking by the beautiful beach was calming and peaceful to him. In the Lord's presence, he wasn't a king anymore. He was just a son, spending one-on-one time with his father. What the Lord admired about Justice was that he would ask the Lord how He felt about things and how he could best serve Him. Justice was in love with the Lord, and he always hungered and thirsted after Him. The King of Kings loved him, and Justice captured the Lord's heart. He was more than just a son to the Lord; he was His friend.

## The Lord Told King Justice to Sow a Seed and Name It

As King Justice was walking and talking with the Lord, the Lord put it in his heart to sow a seed into his prophet. Now King Justice always had a giving heart, and he always sowed seeds for the Lord without the Lord even asking him, because

*The Real Happily Ever After*

the Lord had revealed to him the power of sowing seeds. King Justice knew that this seed the Lord was asking him for was very important, and it was to be done quickly. The Lord didn't reveal to him why, but he trusted the Lord and knew the Lord would do him no wrong. Without hesitation, Justice went and sowed the seed to the prophet and the Lord told him to name it the justice and judgment seed.

## King Justice Paid the Prophet a Visit

King Justice made a visit to the prophet after the Lord told him to sow the seed and to name it the justice and judgment seed. The king really loved and admired the prophet because he had been a true blessing in the king's life. Prophet Jeremiah was always very happy to see King Justice as well. The king told the prophet what the Lord had told him to do. The king sowed a sacrificial seed to the prophet. The prophet blessed him, and the words of the Lord came upon Jeremiah. The prophet told the king that something was coming very soon and that the Lord had nothing to do with this matter. He said that everything would be revealed in due time. Despite whatever happened, the Lord promised him that the victory had already been won, so he shouldn't worry. Furthermore, the prophet told the king that no matter what he heard or saw, he should always stay focused on the Lord and not allow Satan to get the best of him. The king had no idea what the prophet was telling him, but he knew the words of the Lord were true.

## No Matter What, Just Trust the Lord

The prophet wasn't the nosy type. He stayed to himself and didn't get into people's business. He avoided drama in his life at all costs, and his life was strictly about pleasing the Lord and taking care of his family. On the other hand, the

Lord did reveal a lot more things to the prophet than what he told the king, but the Lord had given him instructions to say only certain specific things to the king. The prophet knew why the Lord wanted him to hold certain words back. He wasn't spiritually ready to take it all in at once. The Lord knew his children more then they knew themselves. If certain things were revealed at that time, King Justice probably would have gone crazy and might even have backslid. The prophet always taught the people to obey when God told them to do something. The Lord knew what was best for people. Jeremiah taught his sons and daughters to always trust and obey the Lord, even though they may not completely understand what was going on at the time.

## Prophet Jeremiah Wanted People to Win in Christ

Jeremiah was unquestionably a true man of God and was God's righthand man. Jeremiah truly loved the kingdom because he wanted every single person to be a winner in the Lord. He wanted everybody to have eternal life. He constantly urged the people not to give up on Jesus Christ, no matter what. He taught and preach the word of God whenever the spirit led him to. This man was more than 100 percent for the Lord, and the Lord honored the prophet. Jeremiah taught people how to stay in Christ and not go to hell for anyone. It didn't matter who it was. And he always taught the people that worship, praise, sowing, forgiving, fasting, and focusing were the important keys to staying close to Jesus. Nevertheless, he taught them the schemes and tricks of the enemy and how to overcome the temptations of this world because the enemy always came to steal, kill, and destroy.

## Jeremiah's Dedication to the Lord

The prophet was peaceful and calm in spirit but a soldier. He was aggressive when he was led by the Lord. He didn't care about fame. All he cared about was pleasing the Lord. Because Jeremiah was humble, the Lord allowed him to become famous throughout the kingdom. His heart was pure. The Lord knew he wouldn't use this fame for selfish reasons but would always give glory to God.

Now, Jeremiah was not only a prophet; he was a businessman as well. Being a prophet was Jeremiah's calling, but the Lord had blessed him with gifts and talents as well. That's what Jeremiah taught the people—that their calling from God had nothing to do with their gifts and talents, and the Lord blessed everything he touched.

The prophet was a good-looking young man as well. He had a smooth, chestnut complexion, with the prettiest smile anyone had ever seen, and his teeth was perfectly straight and as white as clean linen. A stallion was he, and his wife had nothing to worry about. Jeremiah loved his wife and cherish her deeply. They had the best of the land and they had three beautiful children as well. He had a happy life as he thought.

## Imina's Insecurities

Imina was not the best-looking girl, but she was far from the ugliest. Her hair and clothes were always on point. She carried a lot of jealousy toward her husband because a lot of the women were so attracted to him, but he paid those hussies no mind. To him, Imina was the most beautiful woman he'd ever seen, inside and out. Throughout their marriage, she'd heard girls talking about her. Sadly, they would remark that the prophet was so attractive and wonder aloud how he could be with someone that looked like Imina. It made her feel insecure, and she didn't realize those girls were jealous of her.

She'd been keeping all those feelings inside and had said not one thing to her husband about it. She didn't even confide in the Lord. But her insecurities caused her to take things out on her husband, and their marriage started going down the wrong path.

## Prophetess Imina's Temptations

Imina had been really mean to Jeremiah lately, and he didn't know why. She'd been complaining a lot, and she felt like he catered to the people more than her, his wife. Jeremiah didn't exactly understand what the problem was with Imina. He did everything possible to make her happy, but she still wasn't satisfied. She definitely knew his calling before she met him, but now she had a problem with it.

Imina knew Jeremiah had placed the Lord before his family, and she started to resent him for that. Some women can't handle a man of God if their heart isn't pure before God. Imina didn't love the Lord as much as her husband did. Back in the days, Imina used to be on fire for the Lord, but something inside of her changed. Truth be told, Imina allowed the desires of her flesh to overpower her spirit, and it became a battle within herself. Sadly, she took her weaknesses out on her beloved husband. Instead of asking Jesus to clean her heart, she allowed her impure thoughts to entertain her. She knew these thoughts were wrong, but eventually she decided to entertain them, and then she let them travel deep into her heart. Soon she was ready to give birth to her temptations. She wanted to experiment, to satisfy her flesh, and her desire was getting stronger and stronger. Now she was letting the world get the best of her. She was curious about the things of the flesh more than she was about the things of God. In her mind, dipping her toe in the water wouldn't hurt, but she had no idea. She made up her mind that she would take a break,

*The Real Happily Ever After*

and then she would return to the Lord when she was ready. She just wanted to live a normal life.

## The Demon Assignment to Princess

There was a specific demon angel, Izzi, that was assigned to Princess Erica all her life. He wasn't very powerful, until Princess Erica made a conscious decision to serve Satan. Izzi's assignment was to turn Princess away from God and shorten her life in order to stop the plans of God. He was called the demon of distraction. Princess didn't know what God had planned for her, but Satan did. Satan knew everybody's strengths and weaknesses. He studied people's gifts, talents, and inheritances before they even knew about their own true essences. Satan was really intimated and threatened by the anointing and gifts that had been place in her life. Princess had no idea that Satan was using Prince Charming to accomplish his own agenda to destroy her. Prince Charming had no idea that Satan was using him as his guinea pig.

## The Demon Reported to Satan

Once in Satan's presence, Izzi bowed before him. Satan told him that whatever he had to say had better be good, or else. He told Satan, with trembling and fear, that his plans were going to be accomplish and that Princess Erica would be there soon. Satan commanded Izzi to come close, and he patted the demon on the head and told him he was a good boy. Izzi's ugly appearance was as a four-legged, hairy creature that gave off a foul odor. He had sharp, pointed nails and sharp, yellow teeth all the way around his mouth. His eyes were piercing red, and all anyone could sense in him was pure evil and hate. Then Satan told Izzi to get the hell out of his face. Moreover, he warned Izzi that if his plans don't go as

*The Punishment Your Sins Deserve*

intended, he would be tortured twenty times worse than what he had in stored for the princess.

## Prince Charming's Wicked Plan

Princess Erica was having a good time and nothing, absolutely nothing, was off limits. Only select people were there, including Satan himself. He was the god of this kingdom. The people there turned themselves over to Satan, and the Lord gave them a reprobate mind. Every sin you could imagine was committed there. Everyone was possessed by demons, and they praised and worshipped Satan himself, whether it was consciously or unconsciously. He was the lord of this kingdom. So this was the moment for the prince to do as he had planned. His protection of the princess ended once and for all. The prince deceitfully got her drunk and gave her plenty of drugs, and she completely blacked out. The prince allowed everyone to have their way with her in any and every way. Unfortunately, while this was going on, there was nothing Kayton could do, because she gave the demons too much power over her life. The angels from heaven could only move in accordance with a person's relationship with Jesus Christ, marked by praise, worship, obedience, and focusing on the Lord.

## The Queen Had to Put the Prince in His Place

As Queen Jezebel was getting ready for bed, she was thinking about how her son had been having these wild, foul parties every other weekend without her. The queen had a problem with the prince because she hadn't been invited lately. At one point, she and her son had been like two peas in a pod. They'd done almost everything together, and she wondered how things had changed so much over the past six months. They'd been thicker than glue, and then one day a change

*The Real Happily Ever After*

had come from out of nowhere. He didn't even acknowledge her anymore.

Moreover, Queen Jezebel was not blind to what the prince had been doing around town. She just hadn't said anything yet. If the prince thought he was in control of this kingdom, he had another thing coming. The queen realized it was time to put Prince Charming in check and let her son know who the master of this kingdom was. She was thinking maybe she'd invite herself to tonight's wild party and give him a surprise visit.

## Jezebel's Slutty Ways

Queen Jezebel decided to make her presence known at her son's party to remind him she was the head witch in charge. She put on something revealing and sexy, making her breasts very noticeable. Jezebel wore a provocative skimpy dress. She wore no panties, just in case she might want to get dirty. She put on her sexy makeup and decided to go curly, with the help of her servants. She put on her seductive perfume, which was specifically designed to make men fall at her knees. It had been made with the help of her friends from the underworld. She put on her provocative red heels, and the queen was ready to make her presence known. Before she left, she asked one of her servants to give her a hand with her black cloak. No doubt, the queen didn't want to be quickly noticed when she arrived at the party. She wanted to stay low key until the appropriate time.

## Jezebel Made an Un-Surprise Visit to Prince Charming's Party

The queen was escorted to the party, and at her arrival, everybody was having a good time. She sat down to get acquainted and mingle with some of the guests while she was looking for her son. Most importantly, the queen wanted to find out how her relationship with Prince Charming had taken a turn for the worse. She remembered that her son loved her dearly, once upon of time, and how they did a lot of malicious evil things together, and they enjoyed it. Now things had changed, and she kind of missed what they'd had together. But while she was waiting, she wanted to have a little bit of fun first.

## Queen Jezebel

The evil witch, Queen Jezebel, was as sneaky as a snake and as evil as a murderer. She harmed and hurt whoever was in her way to get whatever she wanted. The queen believed her beauty and riches were far more valuable to her than love.

Unfortunately, she had no morals and no respect for herself or her husband. This woman was not faithful to her husband, and all the people in the land knew about it. They kept it a secret from the king because everybody was petrified of her, and Queen Jezebel knew it. Without a doubt, she was the most beautiful women of the land, and a lot of the men lusted after her. That was her secret to power. The queen was completely obsessed with power, and she did whatever she needed to get what she wanted.

## Queen Jezebel Taught Young Ladies How to Rebel against God

Queen Jezebel had taught the young women of the land that outer beauty was far more important than what was on the inside. The queen believed that a woman should use her looks and body to get whatever she wished. She instilled this in the women of the land. The evil one also taught them how to operate in witchcraft and how to control, manipulate, and intimidate people to get what they want. She taught them

*The Real Happily Ever After*

that man didn't have any power and that women really run the world. Moreover, the queen taught them that a man's downfall is a seductive woman and her kitty cat. However, the King of Kings hated the wickedness of the women in that land because they were too busy lusting and perfecting their outside appearance and promoting trickery. The women were full of strife and wickedness.

## *Chapter Four*

# Princess Met Satan Face to Face

The two demons dragged Princess Erica before the throne of Satan. All of a sudden, the princess realized these demons were assigned to her on earth too. Besides Izzi, Princess Erica learned that these demons had followed her throughout her whole life. Nobody told her about this because it was already automatically downloaded in her spirit. So when Satan saw the princess before him, he winked at her with the most wicked grin she'd ever seen. As she faced Satan, he commanded her to bow down before him.

Overwhelmed by fear, the princess bowed down before him. She was petrified, and Satan sarcastically asked her how she had enjoyed her life while on earth. She stood there and just started to cry. Satan told her there were no crybabies down in hell. He also told her she wasn't crying when she was living it up on earth when she was practicing being a slut, playing paddy cake with other girls, doing specific drugs, being a drunkard, lying, and stealing.

When the princess heard Satan mention drugs, she told him that she smoked weed and it wasn't a drug. She also put her extra two cents in and explained that weed is a plant and that God said in the Bible that every plant yielding seed is ours. Satan and all his minions burst into laughter. Satan looked at her. He called her "poor thing" and told her he felt sorry for her. He forcefully threw the Bible at the princess and told her to turn to Genesis 1:29 and read it. She read it, and it said that God would give them every seed-bearing plant on the face of the whole earth and every tree that has fruit with seed in it. It said such plants were to be used as food. She said to herself quietly with shock that it was only for food. Satan looked at her with pure hatred and told her that a lot people twist the Scriptures to satisfy their own sins. He said he didn't understand how God made ignorant beings like her.

## Satan Explains How He Got People to Fall into His Traps

Satan even told her that he assigned these demons to her in life to bring her to hell. He grinned at her and told her, sarcastically, that it says in the Word of God that people die of lack of knowledge. Satan informed Princess Erica that he knew everything about her family, while he ran his creepy fingers through her hair. Also, he told princess that he had soul ties in her generations that hadn't been broken yet. Satan revealed to princess that these demons had been following her family linage for decades and that he owned her.

Furthermore, Satan mentioned that he studied them and knew all of their weaknesses and strengths. Last but not least, he mentioned that he did this to everybody on earth to destroy them and to make sure they didn't return to God. He laughed and told Princess Erica that a lot people on this earth were just plain stupid. They had a lack of knowledge about the spiritual world.

## Satan Told Princess about Herself

Sarcastically, Satan reminded Princess that, once upon a time, she'd known the Word, but she obviously didn't want Jesus Christ. Satan and his minions laughed once again. After that, Satan told Princess she was his forever. He told the guards to take her to her cell, and she trembled with fear.

While the demons dragged her harshly to her cell, she was screaming for Jesus. They violently threw her on the floor and told her she wasn't calling for Jesus when she was acting like a complete whore and satisfying all her desires while on earth. The demons both kicked her in the cell and told her that what they'd done to her on earth was nothing compared to what they were about to do to her.

One of the demons licked her whole face with his reptilian tongue and told her to get ready. Princess Erica ran to the corner in complete shock. Balled up in the corner, she just wept and silently pleaded for Jesus to save her.

## Prince Eric's Curiosity

Prince Eric knew there was something peculiar about the woods. He'd also noticed a changed in his sister since she'd been going on those special trips every other weekend. His sister was far from perfect, but he'd noticed some changes in her that didn't sit right with him. He didn't like the way she treated and talked to their parents, and it sickened him. He noticed her attitude had changed; she'd suddenly become prideful. He saw that rebellious personality inside of her, and she didn't use to be that way. So the prince decided he should start spending a little bit more time with her.

By the way, that was his twin sister. He remembered all the times they'd had together when they used to be close. They'd done a lot of things together until about six months ago. He'd just thought maybe it was girl stuff and paid no mind, but now he noticed a drastic change. He asked the Lord about this situation and was led by the Spirit to go on a seven-day fast—no food—with prayer. His father always said fasting gave a person greater power in the spirit realm because they were killing the flesh to become more in tune with the Lord's Spirit. The prince decided to obey the Lord.

## The Prince's Loyal Friends

Prince Eric had two close friends, and they had one big thing in common. They loved the Lord very dearly, and that's what drew them together. Brandon and David were the prince's righthand men, and they were completely loyal to him. They took care of business and always followed the prince's commands. Finally, Eric approached them about his concerns and feelings and told them to go on the fast with him. With no hesitation, Brandon and David agreed to it because they loved the prince honestly with all their hearts.

## The Righteous Prince

The prince was loved, honored, and respected by the king and throughout the kingdom. He was handsome and had a personality similar to his father's. He was tall and very muscular, with smooth olive skin. He was very attractive on the inside as well as the outside. He was righteous and humble before the King of Kings and his parents. He was a just man but carried a lot of wisdom and knowledge. On occasion, when the king was busy, the prince would help solve problems and people matters. On the other hand, a lot of the girls in the kingdom was crazy about the fine prince, and they would do anything to be in his presence. A lot of the girls from other lands would visit the kingdom just to lust after and try to sleep with the prince. The unique thing about the prince was that, as handsome as he was, he was still a virgin, and that was not as common for princes. He had wisdom like his father, and he paid those dust buckets no mind. His main focus was on pleasing and honoring his father and the King of Kings until he found his perfect woman of God.

## Prince Was Put in Charge of Telling Men How to Be Virtuous Gentlemen

Prince Eric taught the young men of his kingdom how to be a man in the eyes of Jesus, not in the world's eyes. Over and above, he taught them how to treat women and be gentle with them, how to be respectful, and how to love the King of Kings with all their hearts. He also taught them that every man is a king and a prophet in his own home. Most importantly, he taught them to follow the directions of the Lord because only He knew the purpose of their lives here on this earth. He taught them how to work hard and how a real man of God provides for his family. He also taught them how to be men of war and how to protect their families. The prince was his father's righthand man.

The king allowed the prince to be second in command of the entire kingdom. The king trusted and loved his son deeply because he served the King of Kings with all his heart.

## The Wicked Kingdom

There was a kingdom in a far, faraway land that hated everything about King Justice. This kingdom was located down in the middle of the woods below. The kingdom was surrounded by tall, frightening trees with no life in them. The woods were surrounded by vicious wolves, poisonous snakes, rats, violent bats, and skeletons. It had a foul smell that made it very hard to breathe. Wickedness enveloped that place, and it was palpable.

*The Real Happily Ever After*

Unless, you were protected by the King of Kings, going into those woods could get someone into a lot of trouble.

## The Lord Was Not Welcome in That Place

It was mostly darkness in that kingdom. There was hardly any sun because the King of Kings was not welcomed there. The presence of evil was so strong in that wicked place that it engulfed the entire being of anyone who wasn't covered by the blood of Jesus Christ.

There was no way to enter this kingdom except through the woods. The woods were completely dark, and you always needed a source of light to make it through. Unfortunately, there was rarely a chance of anybody surviving the woods unless they were led by guards with the permission of the royal family. There was something strange about the guards in the woods though. They wore masks that hid their entire faces, and they were about nine feet tall. The people they escorted in the woods were curious about what was behind the masks, but at the same time you didn't want to know. Everyone knew deep down that these guards were not from this world.

## King Damned Couldn't Take It Anymore

King Damned was miserable deep inside because of all the turmoil he was going through on a daily basis. He'd also been having a lot of sleepless and restless nights. He was being tormented day and night by demons, and he knew who was causing this torture. King Damned now wanted out. Either he would let go of the throne or kill himself. He didn't even have control over the kingdom anyway. The king had lost control a long time ago, and he hated himself for it. People really didn't have respect for him anyway, including his son and wife. His spirit was broken, and now all he wanted was to be loved and respected by someone. In addition, he wasn't even allowed to see his daughter. The evil queen had been hiding Princess Carmina in the tower for three years.

Finally, Damned realized that Carmina was the only one who really loved and respected him.

Over the years, he never really asked the queen any questions. He just basically let the queen have her way. Sadly, he knew he brought a lot of this trouble on himself. Silly him, King Damned did whatever it took to live a certain lifestyle. Now he was paying the ultimate price. Now he realized it wasn't even worth it at all. He'd learned that joy, peace, and happiness were worth more than just money.

## The Naïve King

King Damned was the ruler of this wicked nation. Even though he was the king of this nation, someone else was really making 90 percent of the decisions behind the scenes. The king was handsome, but he was weak and very passive, and the entire kingdom was aware of that as well. Sadly, the king loved his wife so much that he gave her the scepter because he was afraid of losing his rich lifestyle.

The queen used the king and manipulated him in every way. She knew that his weakness was wealth, and she decided to use his vice to her advantage. Eventually, King Damned became a simple man that just sat on his throne, and he was complacent with that, all because of greed. This king acted tough in public, but that wasn't his true nature. In private, the queen would tear down his self-esteem and his integrity in his own home. She would beat him and call him disrespectful names. Regrettably, that led the people in his own household to have no respect for him, and the queen did nothing about it. For years, the king lived in embarrassment and shame so bad that he hid himself from the public. Sadly, this was how he really lived.

*The Real Happily Ever After*

## The Queen Would Protect Her Daughter at All Costs

Queen Jezebel kept her daughter from the community because it was too wicked for her. The princess had no discernment or common sense at all, and her mother knew that society would eat her up like a pack of wolves. The princess wasn't aware of the evil that people would do to her if she wasn't protected. The queen knew that out in the world there were two different kinds of kindness—genuine kindness and trickery kindness.

Queen Jezebel knew the princess wouldn't be able to distinguish between the two. That's what the queen was protecting the princess from. That was the queen's specialty—misleading people.

## Princess Charmina Wanted Answers

Charmina knew her mother was keeping her trapped inside for a reason, and she wanted to know why. She had access to a small oval window where she could look outside, and her curiosity started getting the best of her. She got the best care, and her living space was outstanding, but she was tired of being cooped up in that tower. She couldn't even go outside. That was off limits. She was only allowed to go to certain areas of the premises with protection, but she was still like a prisoner in her own home, and she was fed up. Furthermore, there had been times when she would gazed out her window at night, and she'd seen and heard people having a good time. She didn't exactly know what was going on outside because she was in a tower that was as high as the clouds. All she could really hear was loud music and laughter, and she made up her mind that she was going start asking questions.

## Princess Charmina

Charmina was very different from the rest of her family. The princess didn't worship Satan as they did, and the queen hated and despised her for that. Princess Charmina was gorgeous to the human eye. She had beautiful hazel eyes that just popped out at anyone. And she had soft caramel skin. Charmina was different from the rest of the girls, and she really didn't care about her extravagant beauty either. She was very polite and quiet in spirit, and she didn't have an ounce of evil in her bones. She carried herself with pure love and was full of grace. Nevertheless, the king loved his daughter and he knew that she was special and different from all the women of the land. The queen was troubled in her heart because the king loved her too much, maybe even more than her, and the queen resented it. Even though she hated and despised her daughter for not being like herself, she protected the princess at any cost because the Lord allowed it. One day, she would find out who she should have protected her daughter from.

## The Anointing on Princess Charmina's Life

In the castle, the queen kept Charmina locked up in a high tower, and she was always safe. The queen knew that the King of Kings had a hedge of protection around her, even though being surrounded by pure wickedness. The queen knew in her spirit that she couldn't harm her in any way— not that she wanted to, but she knew the power of God was upon her daughter's life, and she trembled with fear. So she secretly hired women from the poorest part of the land, who privately believe in the Most High, to raise and take care of her daughter. She only had one condition: the ladies were told not to reveal the King of Kings to the princess, or else they would be sent back to the vile living conditions they'd

*The Real Happily Ever After*

endured previously. On the other hand, the queen knew one day she would find out the truth, but she was going to prolong it as much as she could.

*Chapter Five*

# The Demons Were Abusing Princess Erica

rincess was crying out to Jesus with all her strength but to no avail. The demons mocked her and made fun of her and called her every cruel name you can think of. They choked her, threw her against the wall, and ripped her flesh inside and out continually. Princess Erica was miserable in hell, and to see that this was her eternity was dreadful. What she didn't realize was that Jesus was there, and He was only allowing the princess to experience some things for His purpose. He restricted the demons from doing certain things to her. The princess didn't know that she was chosen from the womb by the Father, and her destiny was heaven. Jesus was also going to use her as a vessel to testify and to bring more souls into His kingdom. As the demons were torturing the princess with delight, she kept crying out to Jesus. She was very weak. She refused to fight back. She couldn't fight back. She figured there was no point in fighting, and it wasn't going to change anything for her. For all she knew, she was staying in hell for eternity.

*The Real Happily Ever After*

## The Queen Got a Surprise

At about five in the morning, somebody was frantically knocking on the queen's bedroom door. She quickly woke up. With a frown on her face, she looked at the clock. "This better be good," she mumbled under her breath, and she hurried to the door.

One of servants, looking very disturbed, said there was a girl lying on the shore, and it looked like Princess Erica. The queen looked at her like she was crazy and told the servant, in a stern, confident tone, that her daughter was in bed. In her heart, the queen knew the servant was telling the truth, after the visions and dreams she'd been having for the last couple of days. Also, the queen reassured the servant that Erica was always in bed by midnight, and there was no possible way the person in question could be the princess.

The servant grew very sad, and she hung her head in grief. It was quiet in the room for about a minute, and the queen was trying to gather her thoughts after what she'd just heard. Then the queen angrily asked the servant what she was waiting for. She told her loudly to go get her daughter right this moment. The servant fearfully added that the princess was completely naked. The queen also warned the servants that they better do this discreetly and privately and bring the princess to the queen's chambers right away. Last but not least, she told them to keep this quiet and not to mention it to anyone, especially the king.

## Jesus Came to Princess Erica's Cell

The princess was crying out to Jesus with all her strength, but to no avail. After constantly calling and crying out for Jesus for a long period of time, she decided to surrender to the demons that were abusing her. As Erica was giving up the last inch of fight she had in her, suddenly she saw a small, circular, bright light coming toward her. As the light got closer, it got bigger. The princess couldn't believe what she was seeing. It was her Savior, Jesus Christ, saving Erica from the depths of hell. He was full of glory, and He surrounded her with the purest love she'd ever felt. As He came closer, the demons bowed down before Him and called him Lord. The princess couldn't believe what she was seeing. She was in awe when she saw the demons being wimps before Jesus, and she chuckled. Then she finally knew that Jesus held *all* power. All she could do was bow down at His feet. She didn't dare look up at His holy presence, because she was ashamed. His feet were holy enough. All she could do was stare at his feet and give thanks to the Almighty God.

## The Queen Was Very Hurt

The queen fell to the ground and cried out to the Lord. She was angry, embarrassed, and frustrated at the same time. She thanked the Lord for bringing her daughter home safely, but not this way. The queen felt like she could stay in her room for eternity. All of a sudden, thoughts started going through her head about how she'd been keeping secrets from the king about their daughter. Then she started to worry about her daughter's reputation.

What would people say about her daughter in the kingdom. Moreover, how could she run a kingdom and not tame her daughter. Suddenly, she pulled herself together, and the Holy Spirit told the queen she was not responsible for her daughter's decisions. Then she started telling the Lord that she'd raised her daughter in Him but that the young woman decided to live this sinful life. She continued to cry out to the Lord because she was torn apart. The queen wished she'd just told the king everything from the beginning. Then this would never have happened. That moment, the queen gave

*The Real Happily Ever After*

it all to the Lord. The Lord gave her strength and courage so the queen could be there for her daughter.

## The Princess Was Captivated in the Presence of Jesus

The Lord reached out his hand for Erica to hold. When she held it, His hand felt soft as a pillow. His hands were soothing and warm, and she felt His power. As He lifted Erica up by her hand, she couldn't dare look in his eyes. The fornication, being disobedient to her parents, the drugs, partying, lying, stealing, practicing homosexuality, and the list goes on. She couldn't bring herself to look into His holy eyes. He gently lifted her chin, and he had the most beautiful smile she'd ever seen. Then her eyes locked on His. Once she looked into his mesmerizing eyes, she knew that all her sins were forgiven and forgotten. Deep in His eyes there was power and authority, but at the same time they held love, gentleness, mercy, and grace. He knew everything about her. Her life was completely naked before his eyes. There was nothing hidden about the princess that He did not know. Yet, he loved her unconditionally.

## Prince Charming Was Not Finished Yet

Prince Charming's plans had become successful after all. He finally got revenge, but he was far from finished. After finding out that King Justice was his biological father, he developed pure hatred in his heart. All sorts of things were going through Prince Charming's head. He didn't understand why his father never wanted him to be in his life or why he didn't live with his father. How could his parents keep this secret from him? While growing up, he'd always felt out of place with his so-called father. King Damned never really talked to him or spent quality time with him as a child. He always kept his distance in private, but in public, he led people to believe their relationship was very close.

Furthermore, he was a complete sucker for his mother, and she treated him like trash all Charming's life. In the back of his mind, Charming was thinking that maybe King Damned didn't know anything about this at all. Maybe soon he should pay King Justice a visit.

## Why Did Prince Charming Do It?

While everybody was still having a good time with Princess Erica and each other, the prince spotted his mother on the other side. While she was satisfying her sexual desire with other men, Prince Charming froze for a minute to remember that his mother was always a trashy whore. Also, he remembered how Jezebel taught him how to scheme and to deceive people to get what he wanted. She'd also told him that love didn't mean anything, so he shouldn't ever expect love from her at all. Soon after that, he blocked his feelings and became coldhearted. Basically, he became her friend instead of her son.

They began to have these demonic parties together, and she introduced him to witchcraft as well. Soon after that, Prince Charming became addicted to the lifestyle. That's how his personality came about. Immoral and wicked was he.

## Prince Charming Was Angry That Nobody Really Loved Him

It angered Prince Charming when he found out that Damned was not even his father. Unfortunately, Prince Charming found out by overhearing his mother talking to a close friend about it. The prince instantly became filled with rage. That was when his rebellion started to increase to another level. Later that night, all different kinds of thoughts raced through his head. Prince Charming was asking himself why his father wasn't ever there for him. He wondered why King Justice didn't rescue him from this place. Did King Justice actually love him? Then the prince finally admitted to himself that if King Justice truly loved him, he would have been in his life. He thought, "How can this witch do this to me?" He wanted to get revenge on his biological father for not being in his life. He decided he would take his revenge by sleeping with his own sister. Prince Charming made sure he was going to express how he'd been feeling for all those years and that he felt good about it too. He made sure that the princess was tortured like he was tortured. Prince Charming was going to make sure the king felt every bit of it.

## Jezebel Found Out

Prince Charming walked over to his mother and interrupted the sexual encounters she was having with these men. The prince rudely asked his mother what she was doing there and told her she wasn't invited. With a smile on her face, the queen reminded the prince that she would always be THBIC and that he should never talk to her like that again.

Suddenly, she pulled Prince Charming to the side to see what the big crowd was about. As she was ready to get up, Prince Charming blocked her view and ask her what she was doing. Jezebel violently push the prince out the way to see what was going on. She walked through the crowd and saw a helpless girl, buck naked, on the ground. All of a sudden, her countenance changed from curious to shocked. It didn't bother the queen what her son did to the girl. It was who the girl was that bothered the queen. The queen screamed at the top of her lungs and asked the prince what he'd done. He was standing before her looking cocky, with an evil grin on his face, and he asked her what she thought he'd done. He laughed at her and ask the queen sarcastically what she was tripping about.

She yelled at the prince and was about to reveal to her son who the princess was, and then she caught herself. Prince Charming was already ahead of the game, and he chuckled to himself. Soon after that, Jezebel smacked the princess in the face and told her to get up. She did not wake up. "Oh, no!" thought the queen. She discovered the princess had no pulse either. The queen panicked and told the prince she couldn't go home like this. Quickly, she told two girls to hurry inside and to bring out a sheet to wrap her up. Also, she sent her servants to meet her to tell them to run some warm bath water. She wasn't worried about her being dead because she could easily bring her back with witchcraft. In reality, the Lord did.

## The Three Friends Ran for Their Lives

After they rushed Princess Erica into the house, Prince Charming broke the spell over her friends. They quickly came back to their senses, looking confused, and they had no idea what had just happened. The prince reassured them that they all had a great time and he was ready to escort them to their boats. Not knowing that Princess Erica was left behind, they obeyed the Prince's orders. While they were being escorted to their boats, they knew something was strange. They just didn't know what it was. Even though Prince Charming broke the spell, their minds were still kind of altered from the booze and drugs. When they finally reach the boat, they realize that princess wasn't with them. One of the girls ask Charming where Erica was. He told them softly that Erica would be fine and that they shouldn't worry. He said he'd make sure she got home soon.

Then Marcia sternly told the Prince that she wasn't leaving without her. He told her once again that she would be home soon. Marcia became aggressive and insisted she wasn't leaving without her friend. Finally, he politely stood up to Marcia face-to-face to remind her who he was. That moment, she was reminded, and she hurried into that boat. The three friends started to cry because they figured out something bad might have happened to the princess. What was so sad was that they knew they couldn't say anything to anyone. They were in a no-win situation. They cried all the way home.

## The Prophet Jeremiah Down Memory Lane

Jeremiah was laying back in bed, relaxing, and meditating on the Lord. All of a sudden, he turned to the right and saw on the nightstand, a beautiful picture of his wife and him. He smiled at how things used to be back in the day. Now things were not the same anymore. How could he tell anyone that his marriage was in shambles when he was a prophet? These things were racing through his head. He wondered how in the world he hadn't see this coming.

## Jeremiah Knew He Was Losing His Wife

Finally, reality hit Jeremiah, and he knew he was losing his wife. He cried out to the Almighty with all his heart. He even asked the Lord if he did anything wrong to let him know. For the last couple a months, he covered and protected his wife about her ways. He really did love her, and now she was getting out of control. He cried to the Lord even more than the Word of the Lord came. The Lord revealed to him that he didn't know Imina and that she was not his daughter. The Lord informed Jeremiah that her sins didn't have anything to do with him. The Lord let him know that everyone was responsible for their actions. Also, the Lord mention that he had warned her plenty of times to repent, but she still refused. Last but not least, he warned Jeremiah that she would be exposed and would be used as an example before the kingdom. The Lord asked Jeremiah if he trusted Him. Without hesitation, Jeremiah said yes. The Lord was well pleased, and he comforted the prophet.

## How Did the Prophet Get to This Point?

While the prophet was still sobbing, he asked the Lord why He hadn't saved him from all this mess. The Lord told him that he was going to marry her anyway. Instead, the Lord allowed Jeremiah to marry Imina to show that she wasn't in his plan to be in his future. Justice already had made up his mind about what he wanted to do, and the Lord had stepped back. Jeremiah thought and agreed with what the Lord had said to him.

The prophet Jeremiah ended up opening a school of prophets. Before they got together, he was teaching classes a few times a week. Jeremiah was an outstanding teacher, and he became well known even throughout other kingdoms. Imina attended one of his classes one semester. Once she had her eyes locked on him, Imina decided she was going to do a lock down on him really quick. Every class, Imina was persistent and kind of smothering the prophet. During that time, Jeremiah was saving himself until he got married. He wasn't even thinking about anyone, but Imina became kind of aggressive and intense every class session. One day, the prophet came to Imina in a nice way and told her that he thought she was cool and everything, but he asked if she could kind of back off a little bit. Imina respected his wishes.

## When Imina Was There for the Prophet

Then one day, something tragic happened. All of a sudden, Jeremiah became very ill, almost to the point of death. Imina ended up finding out about it, and she was by his side every

*The Real Happily Ever After*

step of the way. She took care of him and he loved her for that. It wasn't her looks at all that attracted him to her. It was her loyalty and her caring spirit that changed his feelings about her. Jeremiah continued to have faith during this time and knew that the Almighty God would turn it around. Soon after that, the Lord healed him, and his body was completely restored. He fell in love with Imina and she became his wife.

## *Chapter Six*

# The Fall of Lucifer

Jesus commanded Princess Erica to follow Him, and she obeyed. The Lord told her hell wasn't made for human beings at all. Hell was strictly for Satan and the fallen angels that had decided to follow him out of heaven. Lucifer got kicked out of heaven because of the pride in his heart. Satan's desire was to be God and not serve Him. Jesus also told Erica that the demons made a choice whom they were going to serve. He said Satan was named Lucifer in heaven, and he was the most beautiful angel of them all. The Lord had built instruments inside of him, and Lucifer was the minister of music. He was the director of praise and worship in heaven, until iniquity was found in his heart. Unfortunately, when the Lord kicked him out of heaven, a third of the angels followed him. Then their appearance changed into these ugly, awesome creatures in outer darkness. Jesus also told the princess that they could alter their appearance to deceive people.

**Why Satan Deceives and Hates Man**

The Lord also said that when He'd made Adam and Eve, Satan had a lot of envy in his heart because mankind was the only being made in the image of the Father. Moreover, He

*The Real Happily Ever After*

gave mankind power and dominion over the earth, and Satan decided he was going to destroy them. Although they were given a righteous nature, the Lord gave Adam and Eve the freedom to make their own choices. Intimidated by Adam, Satan decided to deceive Eve, tempting her to disobey the Lord. Even though Adam and Eve committed sin, the Lord still gave them grace and mercy and the opportunity to repent, and Satan resented that. Satan and the fallen angels never got a chance to return to the Lord's grace and mercy. They could never again have the glory and the anointing they'd once possessed. Jesus also said Satan and his minions hated human beings tremendously.

Since Satan couldn't get back in the graces of God, he was going to do whatever necessary to bring others with him. Importantly, Jesus promised the princess that if she would always ask for wisdom and be careful of Satan's tricks and schemes, she would overcome.

## Princess Charmina Finds Out Part of the Truth

On this specific day, one of the servants, who was led by the Holy Spirit, ended up spilling the beans to the princess. This news filled the void inside her that she'd been desperately seeking to fill for so long. The more she heard about the Lord, the more joy she had. Princess Charmina couldn't wait to wake up every morning to give praise to the highest God. She would dance joyfully around her room and sing worship songs to the Lord. She didn't care about eating, drinking, or playing games with Patricia unless Jesus was going to join them. The princess loved the Lord with all her heart, all her mind, and all her strength, and nothing or nobody was going to separate her from the Lord.

## King Damned and Princess Charmina

Luckily, King Damned finally found out that his daughter was in the tower, and he was filled with joy. The queen hid their daughter for three years and never revealed it to him. The king regretted his passive behavior over the years, but now things had changed. He knocked on the door, and Patricia answer it with an odd look on her face. He asked if he could come in and promised he would make it quick. She felt very uncomfortable because the king hadn't visited the princess in three years, and she wondered what the queen would do if she found out. Putting her faith in the Lord, Patricia then bowed before the king and invited him in. When the princess heard her father's voice, she ran out to him as fast as she could and jumped into his arms as if she were his little girl.

## Princess Experience the Hurt in Her Father's Eyes

After their moment of affection, he put her down, and his countenance immediately change to sadness. The princess asked why he was so sad, and King Damned explained that it was her mother who had kept her away from him. He revealed to her that Jezebel had been very cruel to him over the years. He apologized to his daughter and told her how horrible a father he was. He asked if they could start all over again. Now, Princess knew that her mother always treated her dad like crap, and she'd adapted to it. She thought it was normal until now. The king was deeply wounded by this, and it broke the princess and Patricia's heart. To see their father broken into pieces was unbearable for them. She'd never ever seen her dad shed a tear, so she knew something was really wrong. Then tears formed in the princess's eyes. She told her dad yes, and she gave him a warm hug. Then the princess told her dad that Jezebel had hid her, saying the king was going to do bad

*The Real Happily Ever After*

things to her, and the princess started to sob. The king told her he loved her and would never do anything to hurt her. They hugged and really cherished each other in that hour.

## King Damned Turned His Life Around

After that, King Damned would sneak in and visit his daughter once a week. Their relationship grew stronger each time they saw one another. Over time, Charmina started to tell her Father about Jesus Christ, and he was pleased. Eventually, the king started to view things in a different light, and he gave his life to Jesus Christ.

The princess, King Damned, and Patricia would sing and give constant praise to the Most High God. Charmina had to warn her father to keep this a secret from her mother, and he agreed. Even though he held Jesus Christ as his Savior, he still had some struggles in his life.

## Princess Charmina's Visions and Dreams

Princess Charmina was enjoying her life in the Lord, and she was floating on cloud nine. For the past four weeks, the King of Kings had been showing her visions and giving her dreams. One of the dreams that stuck with her was about someone capturing her from the tower and taking her away from this kingdom. Not only that, but the person that capture her was a handsome prince. She knew that there was something peculiar about him, but she just couldn't put her finger on it. The part about leaving her family really troubled her because this place was all she knew. This was her life.

## Redemption Drew Near

One evening, Charmina told Patricia about this particular dream about the prince setting her free. She asked Patricia if she knew why these dreams were happening.

*The Fall of Lucifer*

Without the princess seeing, Patricia looked up into the sky and whispered, "Thank You, Jesus." Then Patricia promised Charmina that in due time, the Lord would reveal the things she must know. Patricia reassured the princess that the Lord would never do her any harm and told her to continue to trust in Him. Charmina believed and never mention it again. Princess Charmina ran up to Patricia and hugged her with all her might. Softly, Princess whispered in her ear and told Patricia if this thing was true about her being rescued, she was not leaving without her. Speechless, Patricia was moved, and tears streamed down her face.

## Patricia the Servant

Patricia was a beautiful humble servant before the Lord. She was particularly chosen to watch and protect Princess because that was the Lord's will. Patricia was grateful to be in the castle and not living in the slums. The Lord had been with her and protected her from all harm since she'd been there. She truly thanked Jesus for protecting her from vile men, especially Prince Charming. What brought Patricia to this evil place was her curiosity. Patricia had been kidnapped in the woods, and she remembered it like it was yesterday. Until three years ago, Patricia had lived in the beautiful kingdom, and she missed it dearly. She felt blessed that she was alive, because so many people had died in those woods.

Sometimes she sat back and wondered if her family still thought about her or had forgotten her. Either way, she was excited about what Princess Charmina revealed to her, and she was comforted with joy. She also knew that the Lord was going to use Prince Eric to be their deliverer someday. Patricia had no idea what the Lord had in store for her. The Lord was please with her because she'd passed the test, by consistently

*The Real Happily Ever After*

trusting in Him and giving Him all the glory and praise. For it was Jesus who had brought her here for His plan and purpose.

## King Damned's Secret

King Damned made up in his mind that he was going to boss up, and he revealed the secret to his wife. He had been interested in someone else, and he didn't want to be married to the queen any longer, even if cost him the throne. Besides, it wasn't like she loved him and had a real marriage anyway. He knew the whole time that she was a complete whore, and Damned hated himself for that. What made it even worse was that he was faithful to her the whole time and never once had a desire for anyone else. After being married for all those years, they were barely intimate with each other, because she too was busy screwing everyone else in town. He never expressed himself to her because she was into that witchcraft stuff, and he feared her a lot. As long he was able to live that lifestyle, he was content.

## King Damned Was Fighting Temptation

The king believed it was time to make a change. He didn't care about power, riches, or fame anymore. All he wanted was just to be loved, and this person really did love him. This person treated him like a real man, and it made King Damned feel good inside. On the other hand, it made him feel bad, because in his heart he knew this was truly wrong, but he had to have her. He was in deep lust for her, and if he didn't have her, he was going to lose his mind. He was thinking being with her might take his pain away. Sadly, he didn't realize this would cause more pain than he'd ever known.

Damned wondered if these feelings could be natural, but he had no idea that these thoughts were nothing but the plans

*The Fall of Lucifer*

of the enemy. His lust overwhelmed him completely, and he made up his mind that he was going to see her soon.

## Queen Jezebel and King Damned's Moment

Queen Jezebel look at King Damned disgustedly as she approached her throne. She wanted to know where all this happiness was coming from. Every time he looked at her, he would burst out laughing. The queen looked at him with a mean face and ask what all the rubbish laughter was about. The king told her, with so much cockiness, that he'd found someone better than her. She looked at the king disrespectfully, as if he were a joke, and she brushed it off. Then the king sarcastically told her she didn't want to contend with this person either, and then he smirked. He also threw it in the queen's face that this person was way more powerful than she was. That instantly got the queen's attention and she ask him who could be more powerful than her. King Damned turned to her with a grin on his face and warned the queen that she didn't want to know. She insisted Damned to tell her. He said if he told her, she would definitely tremble at the person's name. He smartly added that one day, every knee would bow and every tongue confess that Jesus.... But he stopped before finishing because Jezebel's eyes look like they were going to pop out.

Plus, she was trembling with fear. King Damned chuckled so hard that he fell to the floor. He hadn't laughed like that in years. Then she rubbed his shoulder and tried to smooth talk him. Quickly, he flickered her hand off him and called her a filthy rat. Jezebel was shocked because he never talked to her in that manner before.

*The Real Happily Ever After*

## Jezebel Gave the King a Nice Surprise

Now it was time for the ultimate revenge, and Jezebel was going to put King Damned back in his place. She smiled at him and told him she had something to tell him. The king rudely asked what she wanted. She told him if she mentioned it, he was not going to like his Savior anymore.

The king looked at her with surety and confidence. He told her that there was nothing she could say or do to get him to turn on his Lord and Savior. She walked up to him in a provocative way and sat on his lap. She looked at him with a funny expression and told him she didn't know about that. Then she started to speak seductively in the king's ear and told him that Prince Charming was not his biological father. On top of that, she told him it was King Justice. Furious, King Damned pushed Jezebel off of him and onto the ground. Now Queen Jezebel got the last laugh, and she asked where his Savior was now. King Damned allowed the queen to get the best of him, and he ran out weeping.

*Chapter Seven*

# The Shame of the Queen's Daughter

The servants rushed the helpless princess into the queen's bed. The queen commanded her servants to leave. She stared at her daughter, and tears filled her eyes. She was thinking every negative thought about what could possibly have happened to her daughter. But the queen decided to shake those thoughts off and try to remain optimistic. Then she threw back the sheets and saw that there was something written on her daughter's abdomen. It said, "Everybody enjoyed the princess, and tell Dad I said hello."

She looked up to the Lord and asked Him how worse this could be. She also told the Lord she didn't have the strength to do this on her own, and she needed Him at this hour. The queen bent over her daughter and kissed her forehead with sorrow. Suddenly, Erica's eyes opened, and she panicked when she saw her mother. The queen gently stroked her hair and told her to calm down, reassuring her that everything was OK. The princess became calm, but when she looked down and realized she was naked, she went into total shock. The

*The Real Happily Ever After*

queen once again reassured her that everything was going to be alright.

Deep inside, the princess felt lost, confused, and embarrassed all at once. Finally, the queen told Erica to get in the bathtub and get ready for breakfast. The queen didn't want to draw any attention from anyone in her household. The princess obeyed her mother's orders and went to take a bath. What the princess don't know was that her mother had erased what was written on her abdomen before she had awakened. The princess walked to the bathroom with her head hanging low in shame and sorrow.

The queen was saddened. Before Erica reached the bathroom in her mother's chambers, the queen walked up to her and told her to keep her head up high; it was already done. She sternly told the princess to trust in the Lord and He would give her peace and comfort.

Princess nodded and said, "Yes, ma'am."

While Princess Erica was taking a bath, she was wondering what had happened to her. All she remembered was being at the party, then being in hell, and then being in her mother's presence. She wondered what her mother knew, but she was scared out of her wits to even ask her mother any questions. She just thanked God for saving her from hell and giving her a second chance at life.

## Princess Erica's Dramatic Behavior

The family was all sitting at the table eating breakfast as usual. This day was an unusual day because the princess wasn't her normal self. She was totally drained physically and, especially, spiritually. She was weak all over, and it was noticeable. Other than being snappy and spoiled rotten, the princess found this particular day unusual. Her behavior was very different, and the king was concerned with her change.

*The Shame of the Queen's Daughter*

The queen kept her composure like a boss, as if it was just another day.

The king and prince looked at each other in surprise, and the king turned to the princess. He knew something was wrong with his baby girl, as she was playing with her food. She had one hand on her face, and the other held a spoon she used to swirl her food. With authority, the king told the princess that it was impolite to play with her food at the table.

Erica sighed and started to weep. She cried so hard she could barely ask if she could be excuse from the table. The king nodded, and she excused herself from the table. The king asked the queen if everything was OK with the princess. The queen smiled and told him that something had happened. Furthermore, the queen encouraged the king to relax, saying that everything was fine and not to worry. Now the king knew something wasn't right with what the queen had said. She was a beast at hiding her emotions but not with the king. All of a sudden, he felt this peace inside of him, and he knew it was from the Lord. So he left it alone for now.

## Prince Eric Visited His Twin

It had been a couple of weeks since the incident, and the princess hadn't been completely herself. Eric noticed she didn't hang out with her friends anymore and she was kind of distant from the family as well. He also noticed that her rebellion had suddenly stopped. Princess Erica's transformation was bittersweet. Eventually, she started to really praise the Lord daily in the town square with a lot of emotion. The king had never seen her like that before. Even though she had changed for the better, the prince new something had saddened her heart. Prince Eric knew something major had happen to her to make her humble herself and do this major turnaround.

*The Real Happily Ever After*

For the princess, humility and quietness were definitely not normal, and he wanted to find out what was going on.

## Prince Eric Comforted His Sister

Prince Eric finally finished his seven-day fast, and he was feeling spiritually great. He felt revived and renewed and spiritually cleansed. After that, the prince was led by the Lord to talk to his sister. Finally, the prince went to her chambers, and she gave him permission to enter.

As soon as he entered, she jumped out of bed and ran to hug him with all her might. She cried on his shoulder and told him she loved him so much. He also told her he loved her as much and never stopped loving her. He wiped her tears from her eyes and ask if they could take a seat. Eric said he knew something was wrong and that she could tell him anything.

The princess put her hands on her face and cried profusely. She told her brother it was very bad. He rushed over to the bed and leaned her head on his chest. He told her if God could forgive her, then he could too. The princess looked at her brother with shame. She said if she told him everything, he was definitely going to look at her differently.

## The Princess Revealed to Her Brother What Happened to Her

Saddened, the Prince started to weep, and he promised her that he would never look at her differently and she that had nothing to worried about. After she calmed down, she started to reveal how she was sneaking to the wicked kingdom and having sexual relations with a boy. In addition, she was using drugs and getting drunk.

While she was telling the story, she was still trying to figure out how she became naked in her mother's presence. The holy spirit warned Prince Eric that she was only telling part of the story, but he was pleased that she spilled that much. He told her everything was going to be OK, and it was in God's hands. They said a prayer together and the Prince left. If the princess had told him everything before the Lord led him to fast, he would have gone ballistic, thinking only with his flesh. When the Lord led someone to fast and pray, it was definitely for a reason.

## The Princess Was Revisiting the Tragedy of Her Past

Princess Erica had been tossing and turning in her sleep and had been restless for a couple of days. Memories were trying to come back to her about what had happened the last night she was with the prince on bedrest. So the princess decided to relax on the patio and enjoy the night view. While she was on the patio, she overheard the servants in the room whispering about her and about how she got brutally raped, and they talked about what was written across her stomach. They said she was a rotten slut anyway and that she'd shamed the king. Moreover, they mention that she was never like her mother, and they giggled and went on their way. Those words pierced Erica's heart, and she wept bitterly. She felt scared and ashamed. How could the prince allowed this to happen to her? Most importantly, she really felt bad for her father, the king. The princess continued to cry until she dosed off. In her dreams, she saw herself on the floor, naked, with everybody surrounding her. This wasn't new to her because she allowed the prince to do whatever he wanted to her, but this time was different. As she invited him to have her, he looked at her in disgust and told everybody to enjoy her. Then people started to take off their clothes and hold her down to enjoy themselves, and she was screaming with all her might. She begged her Prince Charming for help, but he just gazed at her

*The Real Happily Ever After*

with the evilest grin she'd ever seen. She was screaming with all her might, begging for the prince to help and not to let them do this to her. She yelled with hurt and told the prince that she thought he loved her. The next thing she knew, she woke up when she felt cold water on her face. Once again, she was waking up right next to her mother.

## The Queen's Advice to Her Daughter

Princess Erica shyly looked at her mother with embarrassment and ask her what happened. The queen smiled, holding her daughter's hand, and asked her who Prince Charming was. The princess looked at her with surprise and asked how she knew about him. Her mother told her she must have been dreaming and that she'd called out his name for help. Erica dropped her chin, but the queen lifted it again.

Erica said she'd heard the two servants saying awful things about her. The queen quickly called for the servants to apologize. The two servants dropped to their knees and begged the princess for mercy. The queen stared at them fiercely and told them to kiss her feet. The queen warned them what would happen if she ever heard them speak ill of her daughter again. They hurriedly left.

The princess told her mom that she definitely knew she was a woman of God but that she still had a streak of 'hood in her. They both laughed heartily. Then the queen smiled at her daughter and asked if Prince Charming was her boyfriend. Then princess put her head back down and said she didn't want to talk about it.

The queen kissed her on the forehead and reassured her that she could tell her anything, no matter what. She spoke softly and explained to Princess Erica that there was no true happily ever after unless you accepted Jesus Christ as Lord and Savior to spend eternity with Him. The queen caressed her daughter's face and explained that "happily ever after" stories are not real on this earth. She said this life was only for a short moment, but as long as we have Jesus, He will see us through it. She also mentioned that there were going to be heartaches and pains at times, but that didn't mean the princess couldn't have joy and the peace of the Lord within her heart. Then the queen politely walked out of the room.

## After King Justice Found Out about His Daughter

The day after the queen revealed their daughter's experience to King Justice, he decided not to attend family brunch. At the dinner table, there was total silence. The prince knew that his parents didn't think he knew what had happened to his beloved sister, and he wanted to keep it that way.

The king just wanted to spend time by himself. As he was meditating on the Lord, suddenly, everything that had been revealed to him was coming together. The king remembered that the Lord had told him to sow a major seed. Then he remembered that the Prophet Jeremiah had warned him about something that was going to take place and that he shouldn't worry. After he thought about everything, tears began to stream down his face. Then he fell on his face before the Lord and just began to praise Him and thank Him for everything He had done in his life. The king trusted the Lord with all his heart, but he was saddened by how things had gone down. He thought about what happened to his daughter. He desperately cried out to the Lord and asked why that had to happen.

No father wants to see his daughter brutally hurt by others and by a man she shouldn't have been with in the first place. With pain in his heart, he asked the Lord what he'd done to deserve having his family destroyed like that. With tears

*The Real Happily Ever After*

streaming down his face, he told them that there is no happily ever after on this earth—only in heaven.

Then the angel Gabriel appeared to King Justice in a vision. The angel revealed to the king that he shouldn't worry and that all things were working for his good. He also said the king's daughter was going to become a mighty woman of God. The Lord then reassured the king that his family would be restored, and he'd have peace, love, and joy like never before.

## Prince Eric was Upset by What He Found Out

The prince had overheard the servants saying that his twin sister had been brutally raped. That stuck in his head. Then he heard his sister mention Prince Charming. Prince Eric was shocked and confused. Later, when everybody had left his sister's presence, he went to visit her again.

She was very pleased to see her brother. As he sat down, his demeanor was not mean but very serious. He knew she'd been through a lot a pain, and he only wanted to ask about Prince Charming. He remembered her telling him about having sexual relations with a boy, but she'd never mentioned the name. He asked her if Prince Charming had done this to her, and she said she didn't know. Prince Eric put his hands on her shoulders and asked her if Prince Charming had been present when these things happened to her.

Head bowed in shame, she told him she didn't know. Then she told him she wasn't sure. She said she was confused. He laid her back down and told her there was nothing to worry about and to relax. He started to leave with a look of vengeance on his face. Princess Erica sat right up in bed and pleaded with him not to go there. With his back to her, he stopped and stared at the door. He told her good night and left.

*The Shame of the Queen's Daughter*

## Time for Prince Eric to Make His Move

That very night, Prince Eric told Brandon and David about the situation, and they were down for helping him in whatever way he wanted. He told them they were leaving in three days to go into that wicked kingdom. Even though they'd recently finished that seven-day fast, the prince commanded them to do two straight nights and to pray without ceasing. The next day, he paid a visit to the prophet. He sowed a major seed in his ministry. It was the Psalms 105:24 seed: "The Lord Shall increase me greatly and make me greater than my enemies." His Father and the Prophet taught him the four secrets of sowing. First, giving to the Most High God is the highest act of worship. Second, you can sow your way out of things. Third, always name your seed. Fourth, when a person sows into the prophet, it shows that you can trust the Lord with every area of your life.

The prophet Jeremiah blessed him, and the word of the Lord came to him. The Lord reveal to the prophet that the battle was already won. He was instructed to tell the prince to go forth. Jeremiah was usually not nosy, but he had to ask the prince if everything was all right. Eric reassured him that everything was great, and he rejoiced as he left. Prince Eric said to himself, "War is on."

To be continued...

# Author's Note

*I* don't know what type of path you're on with Jesus, but one thing I do know is that He loves you very much. Come to Him as you are, accept Him as your Lord and Savior, and let Him do the rest. He is the only one who's going to be there for you, no matter what, even when people fail you. Whatever you're going through, He will give you peace and rest in Him. Get to know Him better by spending time with Him. He wants a relationship with you!

## A Repented Sinner Through the Father's Eyes
Lord, how can you love someone like me
A sinner! that brought You pain and misery.
Treacherous! Unrighteous Immorally.
A backslider! Deceit in trickery.
Help, I am distorted mentally.
I am drowning in my dirt,
I am rapture with the hurt,
I don't want to be bound;
I am breaking this curse.

Ashamed! Of my faults and my history,
My heart is torn and broken bitterly.

*Author's Note*

Child, it's easy to love someone like you
A treasure! That's made in my image, my precious jewel.
Flawless! Before you enter your mother's womb.
A flower! Blossoming beautifully when it blooms.
Rest in Me! Is the one important rule.
Then the dirt will decease,
Then your hurt will decrease,
If you focus on Me,
Then your faith will increase.
Restore! Change your life, your attitude.
Your heart will heal back to pieces, properly soothed.

Look in me!
Look through me! It's terrifying.
My sins outstretch above the sky, not satisfying.
The suffering in this life, tired of crying.
The battle between good and evil, tired of fighting.
Depression has taken over, feel like I'm dying.
The wicked ways of this world are petrifying

Change me, so my sins can be removed.
You are the one I want to pursue.
I will try my best to improve;
Your love I want to consume,
The one I want is you!

Look at you!
Look through you! It's glorifying.
The day I spoken over your life, I beautified it.
You are kingship, royalty; there's no denying.
That's why I gave My son to the world, when I sacrificed Him.
When He died for the sins of the world, I finalized it.
Eternal life with me forever, no compromising.

*The Real Happily Ever After*

Giving your life to My son, it's purifying.
Just change; then your sins will be removed.
Then your prayer life will improve.
Your mind will be renewed,
Made spotless and brand new.
My grace will be upon you!

Lord, how can you love someone like me?
I am addicted to this world; my rags are filthy.
A rebel! Committing sins consistently.
Wrong friends, who were a part of my family;
Who prayed on the weak;
Hurt people innocently.
I did people wrong;
I've been in this too long.
Whoa! I'm living dangerously on the surface.
Wrong roads, living recklessly imperfect.
I terribly dishonored You, caused You a disservice.
Covering up my sins, hiding behind the curtains.
Deceiving people, like my life was picture-perfect.
Temporary happiness! Lord, I don't deserve this.
But deep inside, my heart was hurt and deeply burdened.
With bitterness, unforgiveness, and sickly hurting.
I am ready to serve you, Lord; a different person.
I surrender all; this lifestyle just ain't working.

Loving you is so easy and naturally.
Just turn to me; filthy rags will be made clean.
My angel, I adore and am so deserving.
My pure joy, my heartbeat, you're more than worth it.
Invite me to be your heavenly Father.
I take you all the way higher.
I will fulfill all your desires.

*Author's Note*

This love will never expire.
Be your healer and provider.
Greatness, My plan, my special purpose.
My son died for you; gratefully, you were purchased.
A diamond in disguise, wonderfully refurbished.
Created in the palms of My hands, you are never worthless.
Heaven is your destiny; there is no reversing.
Peace in me; removes your stress and all your burdens.
Just trust in me, your life free from all your worries.

The way You look upon me is so amazing.
That's why Satan and his minions cannot embrace it.
I am made in Your beautiful image; they can't contain it.
So they use people to destroy me; it's so degrading.
I'm speechless; there's nothing that I can say.
I was blindsided; that area was shaded grey.
I misunderstood You, the only one to blame.
This spiritual walk is no joke, changing the game.
I was always worried about other people's approval.
I thought I can be loyal to both, try to stay neutral.
You open my eyes to the truth; Lord, this was useful.
There was nothing real all along, fake and unfruitful.
They kept me away from Your love, hateful and brutal.
I am glad that I came to You; this was valid and crucial.
Now, seeing me the way You see me,
My love for You quadrupled.

CPSIA information can be obtained
at www.ICGtesting.com
Printed in the USA
BVHW061746111022
649159BV00014B/1121